spirited
exuberant
colorful
open-minded
GENEROUS
Heroic HELPFUL
peace
BRAVE
effervesce
visionary
Patient
inter
OPTIMISTIC
Sincere
inventive
polite
HUNGRY

TO:

_____

FROM:

_____

humble
PEACEFUL
mindful
persistent
EXUBERANT
Helpful
Vivacious
ACTIVE
EISTY
READY
Adventurous
Loving
Surprising
CREATIVE
Reverent
GREGARIOUS
INTUITIVE
inventive

Dedicated to Stefani Germanotta
and who she became.

— P.H.R.

Library of Congress Cataloging-in-Publication Data available
ISBN 978-1-338-57231-5
10 9 8 7 6   21 22 23 24
Printed in China   62
First edition, March 2020
The text type and display are hand-lettered by Peter H. Reynolds.
Reynolds Studio assistance by Julia Young Cuffe
Book design by Patti Ann Harris and Doan Buu

PETER H. REYNOLDS

Be You!

ORCHARD BOOKS

AN IMPRINT of SCHOLASTIC INC.

You were born to

Be

so many things.

thoughtful HOPEFUL FUNNY CURIOUS
spirited
exuberant colorful Loving
open-minded moody
GENEROUS
Heroic HELPFUL
effervescent
Patient
OPTIMISTIC
inventive
HUNGRY
ACTIVE
mindful
persistent
EXUBERANT
Helpful PEACEFUL READY
FEISTY
Loving Surprising
CREATIVE Adventurous
Reverent inventive
GREGARIOUS INTUITIVE

My wish for you—
no matter where your journey leads—
is for you to always...

Be
YOU!

Be
ready...

...to take
that next step
toward
being an
amazing
human
being.

Be
curious.

Turn every stone,
ask every why,
and keep digging deeply.
Discover your own answers.

Be
adventurous.

Live a big life!
When you are ready,
step outside your comfort zone.
Bravely explore new paths
and see where they lead you.

Be
connected.

Find kindred spirits.
Be with those who make you feel
like the real you.

Keep going,
never stop.
Keep going,
never stop.
Keep going,
never stop.

Be
different.

Be silly. Be quirky. Be odd.
Be unique. Be weird. Be colorful.
Be okay with being different.
Be just the way you are.

Help those around you
to be themselves. Listen.
Then listen some more.
Learn more about who they are.

Be

brave.

Try new things.
Take a deep breath
and plunge forward
into new experiences.
It gets easier every time you try.

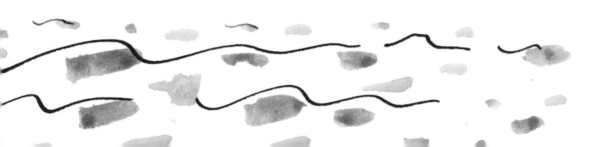

Be

your own thinker.

Think for yourself and
set your own unique course.
It isn't always easy,
but you'll be heading
in the direction of YOU.

Be

okay being alone.

Take time to be on your own.
Hear your own thoughts —
your inner voice.
Listen to your heart.

Be
patient.

Being more you takes time.
Take a deep breath. Relax.
Let your future unfold at its own pace.
It will be worth the wait.

Be

okay reaching out
for help.

When you need a helping hand,
a compassionate ear,
an encouraging word...
reach out.

As you voyage out into the world, remember...

...no matter what,
you will always

be loved.

You are ready.
So...go ahead...BE YOU.
Be very, very YOU!

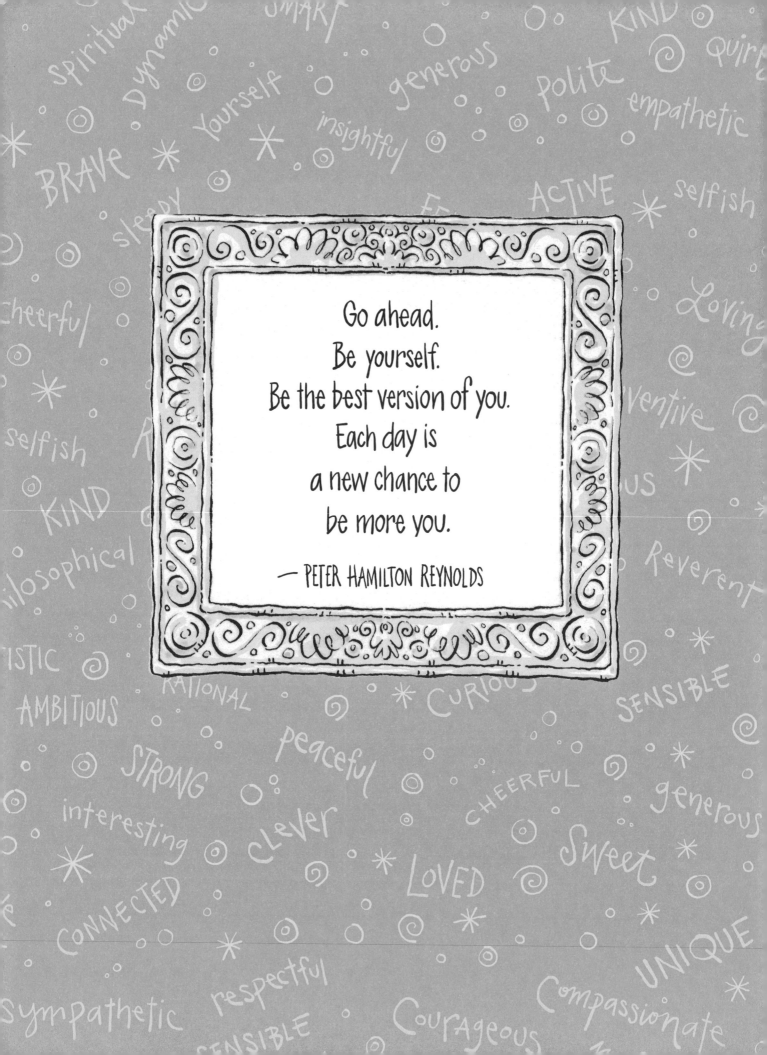

Go ahead.
Be yourself.
Be the best version of you.
Each day is
a new chance to
be more you.

— PETER HAMILTON REYNOLDS